FROM BOULDERS
TO PEA GRAVEL

FROM BOULDERS
TO PEA GRAVEL

Nicki Dawn

FROM BOULDERS TO PEA GRAVEL

iUniverse books may be ordered through booksellers or by contacting:

iUniverse
1663 Liberty Drive
Bloomington, IN 47403
www.iuniverse.com
1-800-Authors (1-800-288-4677)

Scriptures marked as "(CEV)" are taken from the Contemporary English Version Copyright © 1995 by American Bible Society. Used by permission.

ISBN: 978-1-5320-8025-8 (sc)
ISBN: 978-1-5320-8026-5 (e)

Print information available on the last page.

iUniverse rev. date: 02/10/2020

DEDICATION

This book is dedicated to my children. Thank you for showing me perseverance and determination. To my ex-husband, thank you for all of your selfless gifts of love through every struggle. To my family, thank you for always being loving and supportive in everything. To all of my friends, thank you for your prayers and guidance, without judgement, along this journey.

CONTENTS

INTRODUCTION

"But the Father will be with me, and I won't be alone. I have told you this, so that you might have peace in your hearts because of me. While you are in the world, you will have to suffer. But cheer up! I have defeated the world."

John 16:32

Every day we are faced with mountains to climb, hurdles to leap, and boulders to crush. But through faith, we can be sure that each obstacle that we encounter can be overcome. Every trial and tribulation in our lives is never dealt with alone. We may not know what path we are supposed to walk, but we can be rest assured that whichever path we choose, we can walk it with confidence knowing that we are never alone.

CHAPTER 1

WHEN THE WORLD CRUMBLES BENEATH YOUR FEET

"We often suffer, but we are never crushed. Even when we don't know what to do, we never give up. In times of trouble, God is with us, and when we are knocked down, we get up again."

Corinthians 4:8-9

I sat outside my home with tears rolling down my face as I watched the realtor leave with potential buyers. It was not my choice to move. I had lost both my husband and my job within six months of each other. I had no idea where I was going. I had no idea what I was supposed to do. I had literally hit my rock bottom. At that moment, I turned to my friend and said, "One day, I will tell my story. I don't know where I am going or how I am going to get there. But God is telling me right now that I am going to share my story and this experience will guide someone else through their struggles too." He looked at me bewildered. The fear was in my gut. The unknowing surrounded my being. But, the hope, given only by my faith, was in my heart.

My life had funneled like a tornado, gathering piece after broken piece, carrying the debris half heartedly and scattering it around as I chased after it looking for answers. Somehow, someway, in the midst of the most fearful time in my life, God found a way to speak through the heaviness that I felt within me. When I couldn't even think of a way to pray anymore for the events that continued to unfold in my life, He was telling me that I was going to tell my story. I couldn't believe it myself. But I somehow knew deep in my heart that everything that I was going to face was going to be okay. For weeks on end, I had literally raised my hands in the air and said "God, this is more than I can handle on my own. I turn my hands over to you. Take this burden from us. '' His response was "You will share your story"!!!!

"I pray to you Lord! Please Listen. Don't hide from me in my time of trouble. Pay attention to my prayer and quickly give an answer."

Psalm 102:1-2

In my own words, that is what I was asking of Him. I wanted for Him to relieve me from the burdens that continued to fall upon me. I wanted Him to give me the strength to find the answers for a corrective plan of action. I knew that only He could give me salvation!

My world began to unravel that summer when my marriage had failed. I was left with a house, three children, a mountain of bills and daily living expenses.

I found myself in over my head financially with my part-time job. I began to struggle medically after my ex-husband left. With the increased stress of everything, my symptoms worsened. I plummeted in weight loss. Losing five to six pounds per week, my doctor sent me to a specialist after specialist in search for some answers. My dizziness and migraines became worse and my neurologist continued to adjust my medications and repeat expensive medical testing. It became increasingly difficult for me to go to work and perform the duties that I needed to on a daily basis and then come home and care for my children at the end of the day. My fatigue level was overwhelming. I was exhausted after working just a five hour day. My team of doctors worked together to prevent my condition from impeding my life as much as possible, and my new specialists continued to educate me on their new found findings.

"Losing self-control leaves you as helpless as a city without a wall."

Proverbs 25:28

As I continued to search for answers, remembering who was really in control of the situation was not the easiest thing for me to do. I felt weak and weary, and I struggled to control my symptoms. The Bible tells us in Matthew 6:34 *"Don't worry about tomorrow. It will take care of itself. You have enough to worry about today"*. Often times, I think we look at tomorrow before we even think about today. We have a tendency to look at what may come, what may happen, how we might control the upcoming events about to unfold before us. But God did not intend for us to do that. He already has a plan for tomorrow. Just because we may not see it, does not mean that it is not already mapped out for us. It is imperative that we remember that we cannot do anything about yesterday and we cannot do anything about tomorrow. Today is the only day that we are promised. Today is our gift, our present, and our chance to make a difference.

The Scriptures throughout the Bible talk of how Jesus healed the blind, the invalid, the weak, and so on. The faith of those who sought Jesus for healing were radiating and focused on the only person who could heal them. Followers would travel miles in hopes of just being able to see Jesus himself and to be in his presence. There was no doubt in their hearts that Jesus would heal and restore them. People no longer have to travel far and wide just to seek Him. He is right here. All we have to do pray. He is always ready to listen and His blessings are already set in motion. He told us in his word that our faith has already healed us. Jesus said himself in John 20:29 *"blessed are those who have not seen and yet have believed."* Just because we cannot see him, doesn't mean he isn't there. It is important for us to reach out and connect with him so that we can have an intimate relationship with him. I realized that once I began to walk and heal my spiritual being, my physical being also began to get well! Night and day, I would pray for a renewed strength. I prayed for him to restore and supply what was lacking in my faith. Although I still struggled with some of my symptoms, I knew that God was looking over me. In my faith, my condition began to stabilize.

"Trust in the Lord with all your heart, and lean not on your own understanding; in all your ways submit to him, and he will make your paths straight."

Proverbs 3:5-6

I began to build my confidence a bit, knowing that I was overcoming an enormous feat. Things seemed to be settling down until just three weeks before Christmas. I was let go from my job. It brought me such ire to have yet another thing thrown at me! I remember asking God, hadn't I been through enough? Hadn't my children already suffered enough? How was I going to provide for them?

I believe that this is honestly one of the most common mistakes that we as humans can possibly make. We often wonder how we are going to make our dreams into a reality, or how we are just simply going to stay parked in one place and provide the comforts that it takes to stay there. We don't ask anyone else how to get where we need to go. Even if someone gave us a free road map, most of us would not take it. We would simply sit still or drive around in circles wondering why we were not going anywhere. It doesn't usually occur to us that in order for us to get where we need to go, we need to put the car in drive and leave the roundabout. Several weeks went by and I was still not able to find full time employment. I had never felt more scared in my entire life. I wasn't receiving any income other than child support. I didn't know how I was going to feed my kids, keep my house, or pay my bills. Very humbly, I went down to the Department of Human Services and filed for food stamps. I had never worried before about meeting our basic needs since my husband and I made a fairly good income together. But here I was walking timidly into that office to ask for help. I had always thought that I would be too proud and that I would find another way to get the things we needed. But a mother is NEVER too proud to feed her children. I was desperate for immediate relief yet determined to make sure it was not an ongoing need. I was told that I had to wait close to a month in order to receive any financial assistance. With the pantry getting low, my pride very thin, I began to wonder if I would ever get the answers that I had been hoping for.

"Don't keep worrying about having something to eat or drink. Only people who don't know God are always worrying about such things. Your Father knows what you need."

Luke 12:29-30

My ex-husband and I decided to sell our home. I had planned on staying in it with the kids, but with a hefty house payment and no income, things looked pretty grim. We put our house on the market just two days before Christmas. Several potential buyers viewed it, but selling a home during the holidays in bitterly cold Midwest winters of ice and snow, and during a struggling economy, did not increase our overflow of potential buyers. To make things more unnerving, I had no idea where we would go should an offer come in for the sale. With no income, and no state assistance, no unemployment, even rent was not going to be an option. I only knew that I couldn't afford the home we were in. Even if I got a job with the same pay, it would have always been a constant battle to make ends meet.

Everything seemed to have uprooted when my husband moved out. My children were confused and apprehensive. I was heavy with worry. I did not want to change any more in their lives than what was already unraveling before them. I was able to speak with the Father of our church in hopes of receiving some assistance with the private tuition for my daughter. I was almost stunned when he asked me if the church could pay for all of it! I couldn't help but cry. This was the kind of immediate assistance that God's miracles show us! Psalm 103:17 says *"The Lord is always kind to those who worship him, and he keeps his promises to their descendants who faithfully obey him."*

When we are sure in our faith and live in his word, we are sure to see immediate results. When we praise Him and lead others to Him, we see His rewards! This was not what I was looking for when I chose to send my children to a school based on faith. I chose to send them solely in hopes that they would learn God's word and so that they may understand their faith that much more. I didn't do it so that I could reap the rewards, but how rewarding it is to know that He was happy with my choice!

I was inspired! This was a break that I needed. This was God's work indeed! I felt uplifted knowing that He was there with me helping me find my solutions. But even though I felt weighted in my middle, like a blanket on a clothesline, I could look at each end of that line and see where God has been and where he is leading me to go. Each knot was tied and grounded by a post and representing something different. The first knot represented my past, the history that I am leaving, printed for you now in ink. The other knot represented my future, slipped precisely, solidly, and tied only by God's word. It reached upward towards warmth and something secure that could only be lead by His work.

I wanted nothing more than to hurry my climb up that rope. The path seemed so narrow, yet full of life. I knew there had to be more if I just remained faithful and allowed God to guide and direct my path. I knew that this was not going to be the only solution to my situation, but I had hope. It was a hope that had been shattered for six solid weeks. Over and over, it was finally being somewhat embraced within me once again. It gave me motivation to keep my head up for just a little longer.

I have to admit, when all was falling around me, I felt very much like Job. Job 14:7-13 states, *"When a tree is chopped down, there is always the hope that it will sprout again. Its roots and stump may rot, but at the touch of water, fresh twigs shoot up. Humans are different- we die, and that's the end. We are like the streams and lakes after the water has gone; we fall into the sleep of death never to rise again, until the sky disappears. Please hide me, God, deep in the ground- and when you are angry no more, remember to rescue me."*

I so badly felt like burrowing into a hole and waiting until God said to me that the storm was over. I wanted Him to say that I didn't have to worry anymore and that at least this particular storm had run out of rain. I wanted to I live life happily, freely, and without burden. I am sure I am not the first person to want that. I am sure there are many people reading this who have thought to themselves that if they could just bury their heads in the sand for awhile, things would surely have to be different when they decided to come back to the daylight. I knew not where I was headed at this point or if I should fail many times along the way. I only knew that I had to keep moving forward. Like a root, at the smallest drop of water, I sought out more. I knew freedom would come. I had a taste of it's sweet nectar.

God promised us in his word that through his grace and mercy, we shall have salvation. We know it. We have read about it. So why is it that we keep questioning it? Why do we continue to question our blessings instead of recognizing that they are exactly that, blessings? Sometimes God will put us on a position of turmoil because that is the only for us to see and receive his blessing. Sometimes we can't see our blessings because we are so used to getting them. Therefore it makes it really difficulty for us to receive them in our hearts and recognize them as His work. We take things for granted everyday. We just assume that we will get where we need to go everyday because of our own accord instead of traveling grace. We assume that we we will be able to wake up another day on this side of the ground. We make plans for tomorrow even before we live for today. We take our time for granted instead of recognizing that only God can say whether or not we will even see tomorrow.

Just like many of you, I wanted to be in a place in my life where every failure was forgiven and every fear was really just a wonder of when I was going to receive God's next great blessing. I knew the storm would soon run out of rain. I became more and more drawn to God's fruit and starved for a taste of what may have pacified my satiety for calmer ground.

"God blesses those people who depend only on Him. They belong to the kingdom of heaven! God blesses those people who grieve. They will find comfort! God blesses those people who are

humble. The earth will belong to them! God blesses those people who want to obey Him more than to eat or drink. They will be given what they want!"

Matthew 5:3-6

I continued to lift my hands and turn my worries to Him. If I may be honest, I had no other options. I was starving for calmer ground. I knew only He could pacify my fears and put my worries to rest. Sometimes we look at suffering and we think that God is the one who is causing our sufferings. God does not promise that we will not suffer. He only offers us the promise that he will walk with us along the way. Often times we suffer only for God to allow us to see us his blessings in those times. We suffer our trials in order for us to realize that God has a plan for us. It may not be our plan, but it is His plan.

"But that's not all! We gladly suffer because we know that suffering helps us to endure. And endurance builds character, which gives up home that will never disappoint us. All of this happens because God has given us the Holy Spirit, who fills our hearts with his love."

Romans 5:3-5

We may think that we have all of these goals that we want to accomplish and that we want to tell. We may tell God that we are here to tell a story. We may say to ourselves that our story is not over. But the reality is that God is telling us to give him back the pen! He is the one who is writing our stories. It is difficult for us to not be in control of our stories. Although we are allowed to make our mistakes and make decisions that align with our walk with Him, the story is ultimately already pre-planned by Him.

I soon became a single parent of three beautiful children at a very stressful time in all of our lives and at a materialistic time of the year. Christmas. My little ones learned a lot about the season that year and the true meaning of the holiday. We discussed the story of Jesus and they were pleased with the small amount of gifts that I was able to buy them before losing my job. My dinner a bit smaller, for obvious reasons, went unnoticed. My two youngest children talked heartily about the countdown to Jesus' birthday and how we would celebrate it. My middle daughter had made a paper chain at school with a daily blessing to do unto others as we counted down until the big day. There was a little less talk about the presents that they wished to receive that year or the reindeer on the roof. It had become a season unto Him and we recognized the day for its true meaning. The Scriptures tell us in 1 Peter 3:3-4 not to depend on fancy things but to be beautiful, gentle, and quiet in our hearts because that is the kind of beauty that will last. It turned out to be the most beautiful Christmas that I could ever remember.

I finally received food assistance from the state about a month later. It wasn't an enormous amount of money, but it was over half of what we usually spent on our monthly grocery expenses. What a blessing indeed! Still very humbling, but God's blessings do not always come in ways where our pride may not get jostled around in the wash a bit either. The scriptures tell us in Luke 6:20 *"God will bless you people who are poor. His kingdom belongs to you! God will bless you hungry people. You will have plenty to eat! God will bless you people who are crying. You will laugh!"* So true it was. Yet another prayer was answered. I knew that there was some help to make sure that my children would get the food that they needed. It proved to be more than enough for us to survive with some creative meal planning.

After several unsuccessful applications for local employment in a very competitive job market, discouragement continued to weigh in heavily upon me. There were several colleges in the area that specialize in my field and the employee turnover in the field has always been very low. A very close friend of mine was in upper management for a contract company two hours away and made me an offer that I almost couldn't refuse. About two and a half years prior to moving closer to our families, I had worked for this company. I had left my job only to relocate for my ex-husband's new employment and to be closer to our families whose health had been continually failing over the last decade. Although the job would mean leaving my family and close friends behind once again. It was an opportunity to work again. Also knowing that it was the work that I left before with a lot of promise for company advancements, was something that I had to consider. I couldn't neglect the past couple of months and the turmoil for which our lives were currently in. I couldn't close my eyes to the fact that this was the only opportunity that lay before me to better my current situation. I also couldn't neglect to think about the massive amount of struggles that I would have to confront if I chose to accept this position. If there were ever a mountain to climb, this was going to be mine. Without a harness, without a net, without my family, my friends, my pride, or blessings from those around me, I reached up. I began my climb with only faith on my side.

CHAPTER 2

DEPENDING ON GOD

"God Blesses Those People Who Depend Only On Him"
Matthew 5:3

M y first priority was to locate a place for us to reside
in. With my house still on the market, it was obvious
that a rental was going to be the only choice for me to go.
My first obstacle was to obtain permission from my ex-
husband to remove the two youngest children from the
state of Illinois and take them back to Iowa. After several
long talks he selflessly agreed that it would be in the best
interest of the children for me to be able to provide for them
and not to live on the state's welfare. He struggled horribly
with the idea that he would not be available daily for his
children because of the distance that would be put between
them. He loved his children. He may have relied heavily on
me for guiding him in their relationship, establishing their

schedule and where he should fall into place with it, but he still wanted very much to be a part in all of it.

My oldest daughter was a bit of a different story. She was a blessing given to me when I was at the very young age of seventeen. I have often wondered how differently my life would have turned out had she not come along when she did. My beautiful pink bundle of joy was why my aspirations to do well in life were immediately jump started. It was like all of my instincts said to wake up and get moving because she is here for the long haul! So that is exactly what I did. I graduated high school a semester early and gave birth to a precious baby girl. Exactly one week later, I was back to work and I have worked one to two jobs ever since. I started college three months after she was born and it led me to my current career. Somedays, I feel like I owe it all to her. Had God not placed her in my life when He did, I am sure our lives would be very different than it is today. He knew exactly what He was doing when He sent her to me. He knew that she was going to be my new purpose and my new breath. Although I was young and parented a bit on trial and error, I never lost sight of recognizing my first born in the journey to where I am today.

I approached my attorney regarding my dilemma with regards to my oldest daughter. At that time, she had not spoken to her biological father for five months. Several years prior, my ex-husband and I had gone through battle after battle with her father through the Iowa court system. Because of multiple contempt of court papers filed against him in Iowa and the fact that my ex-husband and I had paid our small town attorney five thousand dollars to transfer the case to Iowa I had felt fairly confident that Iowa had jurisdiction over the case of child custody and visitation. With that being said, my attorney advised me that if I was sure those were in Iowa's jurisdiction, I was free to remove her from the state of Illinois. I wouldn't need the court's permission to return back to our small town where she had already spent all of her elementary life.

Thinking I had my largest obstacle out of my way I gave my thanks to God. Matthew 5:3 says *"God blesses those people who depend only on Him"*. I was horribly frightened at everything that was unfolding before me. My mind scattered at all of the new decisions that I had to face in front of me. So, I did as the scriptures told me to do. I depended upon Him to guide me in this journey. I would have sworn that I had searched for an eternity for an affordable residence to land our place back into our small community. Every phone call that I made I turned up empty handed. It seemed impossible to find somewhere for me to rent that not only had the space and was affordable enough, but who would also accept my two dogs. I became so discouraged with every leaf that I turned over. It seemed like trying to get to my new/old job was impossible.

I began working at my new job every other weekend to generate some form of income. I commuted the two hours away leaving my children with their dad. It was the first time in their lives that I had been away from them for any extended period of time. It didn't worry me to leave them, but not seeing them or kissing them in the morning and tucking them in at night, was gut wrenching. It was a small taste for the visitation schedule to come. It was almost a sickening awakening of what the future would behold. Weekends without my children, holidays away from them, vacations that I would only hear about were going to be just around the corner.

I stayed with a coworker, who was also my boss, and one of my best friends. We were able to catch up on old times. She encouraged me that the career move would be a great success and would lead to further opportunities in the future. She was a blessing to me as well for all of the small things and her gestures of hospitality provided to me. Staying with her saved me money in gas and commuting expenses, hotel expenses, and the costs of eating out. Her generosity also allowed me to search the area for apartments and houses to rent as she extended her company and input.

"Two are better than one; because they have a good reward for their labour. For if they fall, the one will lift up his fellow: but woe to him that is alone when he falleth; for he hath not another to help him up"

Ecclesiastes 4:9-10

After I continued to fall short of finding residence on my own, I did what we as women do best. I called in "the big guns". If you are a woman reading this, then you will appreciate what I am saying. We all know what the "big guns" are. Relatively speaking, it is all a part of the gossip chain. It was time to let the gals of my history know of my intentions to return home. These ladies were there to help me with my eldest daughter and the start of my self employment. Most importantly, they helped me find my path to having a more intimate relationship with God. I had not spoken to these friends of mine for quite some time. Most of my reasoning for the silence between us was because

I had felt so much shame in my recent onset of misfortunate events. I was so afraid in my situation that putting on a "game" face to show a confidence that I didn't possess inside me was not something that I was ready for. But my idea of ready and God's idea of ready were obviously very different. I began to share the first part of my story, the hurtful part of my story about my divorce that led my life to fall apart. I shared the part of my story that has gotten me to where I am today. I shared the part of my story that forced me to pick up the pieces and move on, to do what my dad always says. "We do what we gotta do. We may not enjoy it, but we do it because that is who we are. Then we move on and we learn from it". So I began to share the skeletons in my closet with the friends of my past. Their concerns turned my embarrassment and grief into a new found confidence. Even though I was hurting, even though I was frightened for all that I had lost and what more I may have had to lose, I felt uplifted.

"God blesses those people who grieve. They will find comfort."

Matthew 5:4

These women, unknowingly to them, were my comfort. I was grieving horribly over all of my losses. I was trying desperately to do things on my own when I had no need to. God placed these women into my life again. They did what they do best and effortlessly. They stayed upbeat. They stayed humble in His word. They put their heart into mine and made a difference again. God was leading me with more blessings. These blessings were the friends surrounding me.

One of my friends happened to be speaking of my situation at one of her daughter's dance functions. During small conversations, she mentioned to her friend that I was struggling to find a place to reside in order for us to start our new beginning. This is where the miracle of the women's gossip chain began its wonders! The other woman that she knew had a brother who had had a hard time selling his house. It had been on the market for almost a year and she thought maybe it would be a win/win situation for the both of us. It came to pass one weekend in January when I was already staying in town. My girlfriend called me on the phone to inform me that this entire situation was unveiling itself. She wasn't sure if this lead of hers would amount to much, but gave me the phone number of this "brother" anyway. In the meantime, her friend had contacted him simultaneously saying that I might be giving him a call. Of course, I hung up with her and called him immediately. He hadn't had much time, only a matter of minutes, to think about the possibility of renting versus selling his house. We exchanged a few questions and answers and agreed to meet late that Saturday evening to look at the place.

"Know where you are headed, and you will stay on solid ground"

Proverbs 4:26

I was so desperate to find a place that I don't think it would have mattered to me if the house were a blaze of fire. I was determined to get my life back together so that my kids wouldn't have to suffer anymore. There was going to be no way that I was going to stop my perseverance. My soon to be landlord said everything I wanted to hear. He offered me no lease, gave the okay for both dogs to come with us, and the rent was dirt cheap. The best part of the whole deal was that we could move in immediately. The place also had a one car detached garage, three bedrooms, laundry onsite, and a partially finished basement to make into another bedroom area. I literally wanted to jump up and down clicking my heels together in relief!

"Ask and you will receive. Search and you will find. Knock and the door will be opened for you. Everyone who searches will find. And the door will be opened for everyone who knocks."
Luke 11.9-10

I needed to knock no more! My search was over! He continued to play out His blessings before me, laying yet another one in my lap that evening. To find a place to rent with a payment cheaper than my last car payment made me sigh in relief! Now that I had made my agreement with my new landlord, it was time to put everything into place.

CHAPTER 3

TAKING THE FIRST BIG STEP

"We depend on you, Lord, to help and protect us. You make our hearts glad because we trust in you, the only God. Be kind and bless us! We depend on you."

Psalm 33:20-21

M y next plan of attack was to get things rolling very quickly. I didn't want to be too haste, but the beginning of the spring semester for the high school was going to start in just nine days. It was important to me to make sure that things went as smoothly for my oldest daughter as much as they possibly could with the transition to a different school. I wanted her to have a clean start at the beginning of the semester just as the other students that had already been attending our small town school. I didn't want her to begin her classes in the middle of the year and struggle to play catch up with the other students.

I broke the "good" news to everyone when I returned

home from work that Sunday evening. No one was very excited about the idea of relocating. My mother was upset that her grandchildren were going to be a longer distance away. My ex-husband was upset that he would not get to see his family on a daily basis. My two smallest children, were not happy to have to leave their schools. My oldest daughter was the angriest of them all. She was a whirlwind of emotions. Her entire world, which she had tried desperately to hold together after my divorce had first began, was continuing to crumble before her. Still, as an adult, with the responsibility to provide for my young, there was nothing I could do to change what had to be done. I couldn't think twice about my decision. It would have been futile. Even though I was agonizing over the issues of changing our lives, or at least the direction of our lives even more, I knew I was doing the right thing. I had to depend on God to protect us. I couldn't second-guess myself and look in the rear view mirror. They say that the rear view mirror is smaller than the windshield for a reason. It's so we focus on moving forward and not looking back. I had to drive onward towards our destination. I just needed to ensure everyone that this was going to be the best thing for us all. I had to let them know that our future was so much brighter with the opportunities that God was putting before us. In Psalms 56:3-4, it tells us to put our trust in God and when we do, we are not to be afraid. Our friends were waiting to welcome us back. Our small town would be home again. As long as we were together, we would get through it and adjust easily. We hadn't been away from everyone and everything too long to forget things or for our neighbors to forget about us.

I could see my words of uplifting hopefulness weigh

very little with everyone's spirits. We were still going to make our move and I was the one that everyone was going to rely on to be strong, confident, and sure of our entire situation. As children, and even for many adults, faith is just something that they hear about. Because faith cannot be touched, or seen, most people cannot fully comprehend what it means. They may not know what it is like to have achieved that intimate relationship with Christ. To know Him and to make Him known to others is not something that they understand how to practice. God meets everyone at a different time and place in their lives. He doesn't care how long it takes us to know Him. He cares only that we continue to make progress in getting to know Him. It was hard to explain to three young children that it was okay for them to turn their lives over to faith in a higher being that they were still too young to understand.

"No one lights a lamp and puts it under a bowl or under a bed. A lamp is always put on a lamp stand, so that people who come into a house will see the light. There is nothing hidden that will not be found. There is no secret that will not be well known".

Luke 8:16-17

This is a powerful scripture. Everything that is hidden in the dark will come into the light. It is up to us to come out of the shadows, repent as children of God, and to let him lead, guide, and direct us into a much brighter future. We don't have to hide from everything that is out of our comfort zone. God will help us to transform even when we feel like everything is falling apart. Our reality is that everything is really coming together for our highest achievements. We are being pushed out of the darkness in order to evolve in life so that we can experience our most high blessings. We need to welcome our changes. I had to keep my own emotions out of the equation in order to receive God's blessing in this and for me to see the secrets that He was about to unfold in our lives. I was the one who God chose to be the lamp stand for my children in this situation. He was going to light our way if only I stayed strong enough to stand up to the obstacles before us. I was who He had chosen to guide my children in this journey as he guided me. I had no choice but to stay plugged into His power. I craved his energy because of it. The more I felt Him, the more I needed Him. The more I needed Him, the more I felt Him. I needed Him like a plug to a socket. Seeking Him became like a drug to me. It was so incredibly powerful, yet with that power came so much peace. I stood only because He lit my way. He was working through me for my children so that they could see that He was there also. As they heard me speak of our future and of the blessings that God had in store for us and the ones He had already given us, He was using me to spread His word to my children so that they could be comforted. As I presented our new journey to my children with the greatest of bright and shining confidence, I pulled every bit of God's energy that He would put into my heart. With that energy, I used it and I prayed.

First thing that following Monday morning, I brought my oldest daughter to our small town to enroll her in the second semester of her freshman year. As expected, she was very upset over the entire situation. We met with the high school administration to register her and complete her course agenda. The courses did not completely coincide from her previous high school and the process seemed a bit grueling. But in order to ensure she would receive proper credit for the courses that she was going to be taking, we had to go over each course objective to compare their similarities. Before the process was over and done with, and really almost before it even began, I started to see a side of my daughter that I had never seen before. A normally respectful teenager to others, soon became that kid that every parent swears he/she will never allow her child to become. She was disgruntled and rude to her new guidance counselor. Naturally, I was embarrassed and apologetic for her behavior. She didn't belligerently call the counselor rude names, but she made snide remarks about not wanting to be there and directed those remarks at the one person helping us. She told the woman she was wasting her time because she wasn't interested in being there. Her persistence made the woman's shoulders slump and it was enough to make me want to crawl under the table.

Now, many of us have children and at one point or another, we find that they are only unknowingly embarrassing themselves. I honestly believed that this poor woman would see that this was another case of poor parenting to an ungrateful child. Understanding that my daughter didn't have much time to process the information thrown at her from the night before, I tried my best to keep my ire in check. I did what every parent reading this book would do though and I did what I am sure every parent has mastered with their children, and shot her with the hardest motherly glare of disapproval for her disrespectful behaviors. It is a stare known by all of our young that symbolizes everything encompassed into just a single look. It has but one meaning. It says "you have tread to the thinnest of waters and should you paddle any farther you will surely drown". Although never afraid of a little deep water, my daughter quickly caught on to my glares and corrected her actions to the best of her teenage ability. She kept a snide look on her face and closed her comments to a grumble of inaudible mouthing gestures.

It amazes me that God has given all animals such a wonderful gift of patience with their children. Truly and honestly, it can only be a gift. To love our young at some of their worst moments in time is an instinct that we as parents have been given to allow our offspring to survive this world while they are still under our wings. Some of the things that you will read in this story, all true, will absolutely amaze even the strongest of parents. The things that we do to follow God's word, to raise our young in His house, teaching them to know what it means to have integrity and faith and love are not always the easiest tasks to accomplish or to overcome. These things become some of our hardest battles to fight.

Ephesians 6:16 says *"Let your faith be like a shield, and you will be able to stop all the flaming arrows of the evil one"*. Ephesians 6:11 and 6:13 states *"Put on all the armor that God gives, so you can defend yourself against the devil's tricks… Then when that evil day comes, you will be able to defend yourself. And when the battle is over, you will still be standing firm."*

He may not have been referring to our children when He sent that message to us in Ephesians. You and I may have never thought that we would need to put on armor to defend ourselves against the devil's tricks that he works upon us through our children. There was no doubt in my mind that war was about to ensue and faith would save me from those arrows. Because we are saved and blessed in God, He is our shield. We can fight all battles when armed with Him in our defense.

I had thought I was already walking through my battlefield, but the war was just beginning. After registration, my daughter had asked to meet with her dad for an impromptu shopping excursion when we returned home. I agreed, thinking to myself that it would be nice for the two of them to rekindle some lost time (if you remember from earlier in my story, she had not spoken to him for almost five months). She arrived home rambling about her shopping trip. She was quick to show me her items and quick to leave the room back to her bedroom to disappear for the night.

Just a couple of days later, with only two more to go before moving day, the day started out normal. Everyone awoke cheery, ready for the day. The kids were off to school without a glitch. I was at home packing things waiting for Friday to come. I received several text messages that morning from my daughter's stepmother. Every time she would send me messages in the past, it was always some form of a ramble about something that was a one-sided suggestion, a dagger of differential opinion, or something of the sort. I rarely responded to her due to the nature of her immaturity. The timing of her messages on this particular day was very interesting to me and I feel like it led to God's whisper in my ear that afternoon.

My daughter too, began sending me messages. They started out about school being out early due to the weather turning sour. An expected accumulation of an inch of ice was to lay on the roads and power lines. Her mood had changed from the cheerful one of her mornings to a mood of anger and resentment. It was hardly due to some course of action or event from the school day. Her demeanor was harsh and directed at me.

She began to TELL me her plan to go home with her dad afterschool, which had never happened in the past. Because of the forecast, I TOLD her that that was unacceptable and I would continue to pick her up as planned. I had no desire to take any risks driving in an ice storm. The normal driving time to their residence in dry weather was twenty-five minutes away. Her temper was set off by her unexpected change of plans. This was unlike her as well. Normally if I would have explained to her that the driving conditions were too risky to chance our safety, she wouldn't have blinked. She had driven many times in bad weather back and forth from Iowa to Illinois and suffered the anxiety of it on enough occasions to appreciate the opportunity to reschedule things when it's an option. But this time was different. I sensed something. God was not just whispering to me. He was yelling at me to take action! School may have been getting out early, but she was getting out earlier than that!

I called the school within minutes of getting a knotting gut feeling in the pit of my stomach. I let them know of my plans to pick her up earlier than their scheduled early dismissal. To her complete surprise, she met me with her cell phone in hand. She was fuming mad! She was telling either her dad or step-mother that I had arrived to pick her up instead of them and that their plans were ruined. I questioned her intentions. She admitted, very openly, that she had intended to leave the school out another door at the end of the day with her dad. Then she was going to "disappear" so that she would not have to move away from the friends that she cared about. She was going to leave me to sit and wait and wonder where she was and if she was okay. Worse yet, her biological father, a grown man and parent to other children himself, was going to participate in such an event. Neither of them had any regard to the worry that I would have suffered if he would have taken her. Neither of them cared that legally he could have been in trouble for kidnapping should their plan had worked out the way that they had hoped. Neither of them was keenly aware of God's whisper into my ear that afternoon.

This began an unfortunate turn of events for my teenager's last few days before our move. She was grounded to my side......literally. She was cut off from her social ties to her friends and to her father and his wife through the use of her cell phone and the computer. Easily enough, the ice storm had taken out our internet for the next couple of days following. I confiscated her cell phone and she was only allowed to use the home phone while I was in the room. It was not the best way for her to enjoy her last few nights at home, especially being a teenager. She was away from her friends. She had no cell phone, and no computer access. I was left with no other choice but to punish her for her behavior. She had openly admitted to attempting to defy me and to trying to run away. I was not going to allow her behaviors to intercept what needed to happen to take care of our family. I was not going to allow her to walk all over me either.

Everything had simmered from the day's events. It was nearing five o'clock, just an hour and a half since all privileges were taken away. I was off of my "soap box" where I stood preaching the difference between what is wrong and right. My daughter and I were standing over the stove cooking up a light dinner of Sloppy Joe's and fries. She was no longer acting hateful and we were going about our evening as usual. The weather outside was laying down a nasty sheet of ice. While stirring the skillet, the doorbell rang. I left her to attend to the meal and my two little ones broke away from their cartoons to eagerly meet me at the front door to greet our visitors. My youngest, honored to be the man of the house at four years old, opened the door. To our surprise, we were gazed at with slight confusion by two police officers who looked as though they had approached the wrong house. One of the uniformed gentlemen stepped back to double check the number on the house before stating their business with us. They smiled awkwardly knowing immediately that they were sent under false pretenses. According to them, my daughter's father had requested that a couple of police officers to go to our home to check on her since he was unable to get a hold of her. She rolled her eyes at the officers and assured them that she was okay. We told the two on duty that he did not attempt to call my cell phone to contact her and we apologized for wasting their time. We also informed them that our home phone was out of order due to the ice storm outdoors at that present time. They said they would forward on our request for her dad to try to contact my daughter through my phone first before wasting the time of law enforcement. The officers then pleasantly agreed to all being well within our home and bid us farewell. The four of us went about our dinner but with difficulty trying to explain to the two youngest children why the police only wanted to know if their older sister was okay in the storm and not anyone else!

CHAPTER 4

STEPPING UP

Because my daughter was now grounded to my side, we proceeded to her soon to be former high school the next morning to unenroll her from her courses a couple of days earlier than we had originally planned. I could not afford to take any risks. We packed our things and were ready to move Friday evening. A friend of mine stayed with her that afternoon and prepared the moving truck while I set forth on an errand to get some documents to my attorney's office. When I returned, he, his son, and my brother were ready to load the truck to get us on our way. My two youngest children were with their dad for the weekend. While my friend's son and my brother began to load, I was pulled to the side for brief conversation. I was told that my daughter had a cell phone on hand and had been trying to hide her texting since I had left that afternoon. This cell phone was not one that belonged to the household. When approached, her story unraveled that her "father" had encouraged more deceitful behaviors by dropping off the phone onto our back deck for her to pick up the night before when she went outside to feed her dog. Satan's temptations in her life were already difficult enough for her to overcome; now she had a parental figure encouraging further deceitful behaviors. I had little time to argue and with the new phone now on my person, I began to play queen bee to my workers for the loading of the truck. Several hours later, we were ready to venture to our tiny new rental on that late January night.

We arrived at the house about 10:45 p.m. I drove with my daughter, who was allowed to bring her best friend in tow. When we went inside, the two teenagers were several steps ahead of me in the tiny eight feet long by three feet wide galley style kitchen. What lay ahead for them to feast their eyes upon was something that I had not prepared them for viewing.

In my excitement to finally be able to land us back home so I could begin to work again, I had forgotten about the condition of the tiny rental that I had agreed to turn into a home. The girls stood bewildered not only at the size of the place which was an eight hundred and sixty-seven square foot, two bedroom ranch with a finished attic and a single bath. The walls were filthy and cracked with several holes in them from old nails. There were large dents and holes in the plaster in several other areas throughout the house as well that would take more than just a small bit of spackling to repair. The bedroom lighting in the flat mint colored room barely illuminated enough light to produce more shadows than a night light would. The light fixture in the kitchen did not work at all. There were no doors on the bedrooms and no shower in the bathroom. The toilet leaked into the basement. The hardwood floors were horribly splintered and needed fully replaced or covered. The place was a mess.

Upstairs, in the finished attic, the stairs were steep, much like a ladder. The room was large and ran the entire length of the house with storage on the east side of the wall. The room was beautifully covered from floor to ceiling in a knotty hickory colored pine. A window strategically placed at each end of the room added additional lighting. This room became my eldest. She had her own space. She actually had her own half of the house. It was dirty and in need of a broom and some dusting, but overall, it was the best room the entire house.

Downstairs, in the basement, was going to be where I had envisioned the master bedroom to go. I had decided for all practical purposes that the two small upstairs bedrooms would be best suited for the little ones. The basement was supposed to be partially finished, however when we moved in, that was not the case. There had been some water damage and the owner was supposedly going to have new carpet and drywall to finish it off within the week. The rest of the downstairs was, unfortunately, horribly creepy. The walls were falling apart and it smelled terrible. There was water damage, a shower that I could not imagine being naked in, and creepy crawly things lingering in small spaces almost everywhere I turned.

This place was a far cry from the comfortable living that I was used to. I was not surprised that the girls were so taken aback by it all. Our last two houses were quite large with plenty of room to roam. They both had beautiful hardwood floors that other people were envious of. There were four bedrooms in each home and finished basements free of things that crunched under your feet. They felt like home. It felt good to be in them and to have everyone over to entertain. There was over twice the space to entertain as well. I wondered as we began to unload everything where it would all go and how it would all fit. I wondered if I could make this little shack a home, like the homes that my children were used to.

"You are my fortress, my place of safety; you are my God, and I trust you." The Lord will keep you safe from secret traps and deadly diseases. He will spread his wings over you and keep you secure. His faithfulness is like a shield or a city wall."
Psalm 91:2-4

I knew from those verses alone that we would be safe and comfortable in that house. Because God is our fortress and safety, He has always kept us secure everywhere we have been. It has never mattered where we have laid our heads, as long as we have trusted in Him. Further in *Psalm 91:14-16* *"the Lord says, "If you love me and truly know who I am, I will rescue you and keep you safe. When you are in trouble, call out to me. I will answer and be there to protect and honor you. You will live a long life and see my saving power."* Nowhere in the scriptures does it say you will need to fend for yourself in this lonely world and fight Satan's demons alone! It says "Call out to me. I will answer."

This broken little house may not have been the answer that someone else would have expected to get, but it was my answer. I saw beyond the holes in the walls and the bugs in the shadows of the basement corners. I saw God's relief to me. I saw Him giving me another chance to face that boulder before me. This place was only a temporary stepping stone in my eyes. It was a brief step as we continued to brace ourselves to climb further up that mountainous rock. It was a momentary allowance to breathe while I set my career back into action. I was certain that all would fall into place as God had promised it would. He never did promise when, just that He had a plan for us and we would be okay.

Close to one o'clock in the morning, we finally finished unloading the truck. Much to our surprise, my daughter's old best friend had showed up just before we were about to head back home. Her friend was elated to have my daughter back in town and was hopeful to be of some assistance in the move. We were thankful for the sweet late night "welcome back" gesture and my daughter agreed to meet up with her the following day after we returned with another load of things. After our welcome home, the girls and I gathered our thoughts and our exhausted moving men and headed back to Illinois.

The following days included more loading and then another entire day of unpacking. My daughter was allowed to hook up with old friends in our new/old small town and was gone throughout the rest of the weekend. I thankfully have always been blessed with a wonderful gift of organization and speed when it comes to packing and unpacking. I can literally unpack and organize my entire house (when there is room) in a matter of two days. Of course, that is exactly what I did. I found a home for all of our belongings, stuffing corners and shelves to their capacity. I first focused on the bedrooms for the little ones so that it would feel like home when they arrived. The two loved their new spaces and took no regards to the flaws of the rest of the house. My bedroom furniture remained tucked to the side the living room taking up over half of the space since the basement carpet and walls were not going to be finished right away. Everything was in the space that it could be for the time being before school began the following day.

When Monday came, there seemed to be little trouble getting everyone off to a great start at their new schools. I wasn't scheduled to begin work until the following week, but ended up resuming full-time hours by the end of our first week back "home". Everything had fallen into place so well. Working again felt wonderful, purposeful, and peaceful. I was completely at ease with how well everything was going with our transition. The kids were enjoying school and rekindling friendships with old pals at both school and daycare. Even my oldest had found herself a new boyfriend within the first week of our move back. She was like a new fish in the sea. The boys were absolutely swarming at their new bait. She totally loved the newfound attention.

I, on the other hand, was beginning to miss my friends and family terribly. They were two hours away and I had grown accustomed to having their voices to reassure me. Although we still talked frequently, I was beginning to feel more and more alone. I knew that I still had the kids with me. But to not have them to confide in, or to be readily available was difficult for me. To know that in order for me to provide for my children, I had to possibly give up my chance to feel those connections was selflessly breaking me. For the first time in a long time, I struggled with my own skepticisms of "what if's" wondering what I would do with the whole situation if I lost my armoured connections. What would I do if it never worked out and I had to explain to my children how I failed them by bringing them away from everyone? Could I fully commit myself to this new journey when my heart was still stapled deeply to old life even though that was no longer an option? These were questions I am sure many divorced people have asked themselves as well. I could only pray that God would continue to guide my heart in the right direction.

I'm sure I am not alone in my thoughts when I say that it never takes much time for our kids to snap us out of our selfish thoughts of "me" and "my" and back into the wonderful world of our parenting reality. There really wasn't too much time for me to wonder what, or how, I was going to handle my skeptical woes, because my fourteen year old teenager had decided for me that there was just no time for me to be thinking of myself. I received a subpoena in the mail stating that I had an upcoming court date the following week over a child custody hearing. The papers indicated that my oldest daughter's father was seeking a change of custody and that she was the one who initiated the idea into his head.

During the impromptu shopping excursion with her dad, the two had met with an attorney and came up with some master plan to get her to stay back in Illinois to finish out her freshman year of high school. She had written a letter requesting the court to grant her absent father full custody so that she could continue to go to school with her friends. He didn't then and does not now reside within the school district, or state, of her old school. He had promised her that he and his wife would use his mother's address (which was in the district) as their residency. Her letter stated that she wanted to stay with her friends and that her dad understood this; she wanted to go and live with him. Wow! Dear God, please be with me was all that I could think.

My baby, my daughter whom I had always altered my entire world around was taking me to court just so that she could be with her friends. I was mortified. I had turned down a higher management position with my company so that we could reside in the small town where she grew up. That promotion would have meant at least another ten thousand dollars a year for us. I had also turned down another position in eastern Illinois for similar yearly wages. I wanted my daughter to be near the friends that she knew already. I wanted her to be somewhere familiar. I wanted to make sure that this time the transition was easier for her than it was for her last time when my ex-husband and I moved her to Illinois. I had thought mainly about her struggles in the transition and I wanted to make it easier on her. I was absolutely sick. I was lost, confused, and on bended knee.

I could not understand how this could be a boulder that lay before me. This was a story that I could only imagine hearing or reading about in the newspaper. This was not a story that I was going to be living. This was not one that I was going to tell. Certainly, this was not one that I was going to write! My daughter had never cared to spend every other weekend with her dad let alone voiced any desire to live with him. The thought, too, that she would go behind my back and do such a thing seemed so surreal. Could all of this, on top of all of the trials that had already tested my faith, really be happening to me? I couldn't imagine fighting another battle. I felt like I hadn't even gotten through my last one yet!

"You can see that Benhadad's army is very strong. But the Lord has promised to help you defeat them today. Then you will know that the Lord is in control."

"Who lead them into battle?" Ahab asked.

"You will!" the prophet replied.

1 Kings 20:13-14

The scriptures say that as long as we know that the Lord, our God is in control. Then we will be able to lead our own side of the battle! No matter how large the battle may seem, it is just a small pebble beneath God's feet. With His strength, I would be able to lead myself into that battle. It says in *Ephesians 6:13 "when that battle is over, you will still be standing firm."* This, again, I had to remember. But I will not lie to you. I was a crying fool. I had no idea how to hold myself together, even with my faith as strong as it was.

CHAPTER 5

FROM BOULDERS BACK
TO THE MOUNTAIN

I met with my attorney right away. My parents were again a blessing of generosity to loan me the money for the retainer fee. My attorney gave me hope that the case would fizzle out and that there was no way that any judge would take a child away from a perfectly good parent just because she moved to provide for her children. He also assured me that the judge would think that accepting employment where my daughter was raised for the majority of her elementary life was also an excellent option to have available to me. The fact that her dad had been primarily absent in her life would weigh in very heavily on the judge's decision as well. I left feeling hopeful and almost relieved that this whole situation was nothing but some silly teenage graffiti in my history book.

Piles of court records were gone through from prior years. Files that on multiple occasions he was found in contempt of court for various reasons that for the sake of my daughter, I will not name in this book. Although my ex-husband and I had paid out a small fortune to have our case transferred to Iowa, according to my new attorney, every attempt that was made fell flat on its face. Our old attorney mistakenly never followed through on his end to get the task done. I was stuck. I had officially removed my daughter from the state of Illinois, unknowingly, without the court's permission. The first strike was automatically against me for not doing my homework prior to my move. Surely, this oversight would be taken into account by the judge after he saw all of the prior attempts to have the case transferred right? It was not likely that someone not familiar with the system would know that it never went through.

Alone, I drove into town to face the bull by the horns. My daughter had stayed with her dad the night before, conveniently, so the ride to town was my own silent discomfort. It was awkward for me to sit outside the courtroom and have my daughter wander about giggling immaturely with them as if they were all at some basketball game hanging out on the bleachers. They were loud and disrespectful even inside the courtroom. They took no regard to the fact that it was a place to assume respect. The bailiff did finally quiet them before the judge appeared.

About mid-way through the hearing was when I knew. I knew that there was no chance for me to have anymore hopes that the judge would consider my mishap. He ruled that she was to finish out her freshman year in Illinois and another hearing would be set at a later time for the child custody case. He also made note that he was fully aware of the fact that neither parent resided within the district, and that her custodial parent lived two hours away from the district. He didn't care how she got to and from school every day. She could commute. She could stay with friends and family. It was my feeling that he could care less if she stayed in a homeless shelter, as long as she got to that particular school every day. It was my responsibility to immediately re-enroll her back in the school that everyone else felt like she belonged.

I couldn't believe what I was hearing. How was all of this supposed to happen? How was I going to afford to commute her two hours to school every day, then drive two hours back to work, then leave work earlier to drive another two hours to pick her up and drive another two hours back home? It would literally cost me $75 per day in gas money just to commute her for school. Then of course, there was the matter of my two smallest children. What was I supposed to do with them? Would they really have to be at the sitters at 5:00AM every morning just so I could take her to school? What would happen to their school day? What happened if they forgot something or they became ill and I was so far away? Would I really have to be that mom that was away from her children for twelve hours a day? I had never even worked longer than their school day. I have always made myself available so that I could be there for them every second that my children might need me. The magnitude of the entire situation played out to be way more than I could even breathe in. I wanted to pray, but didn't know where to begin. I could feel God telling me not to fight the arms around me because He was there. But was this really what He wanted for us? I knew He wanted me to hold onto His word and not lose my composure, but I couldn't help myself. I was but a puddle of worry, and loss. But I did not blame our Lord.

"We bring nothing at birth; we take nothing with us at death. The Lord alone gives and takes. Praise the name of the Lord!"

Job 1:21

It is so easy for us in our weakest times to blame God for our problems and our misfortunes. Especially when we, like I, have no idea what we may have ever done to deserve such misfortunate events to continuously occur in our lives. What we must remember is that God never promised that Satan would not enter our lives. He only promised that He would be there with us when he did. So, with my heart in my hand, and God in my heart, I prayed.

Psalm 121.

The Lord Will Protect His People.
I look to the hills!
  Where will I find help?
It will come from the Lord,
Who created the heavens
  And earth.

The Lord is your protector,
And he won't go to sleep
  Or let you stumble
The protector of Israel
Doesn't doze
  Or ever get drowsy.

The Lord is your protector,
There at your right side
  To shade you from the sun.
You won't be harmed
By the sun during the day
  Or by the moon at night.

The Lord will protect you
And keep you safe
  From all dangers.
The Lord will protect you
Now and always
  Wherever you go.

I prayed for God to just be with me while I sorted through my struggle and made out my game plan for how I was going to attack the situation head on. I prayed that He would protect me as I lead myself into a battle that I knew was about to become a war. With a VERY deep breath, I did what I was told to do.

Within the next few days, I attempted to re-enroll her back in her former high school. I had previously contacted her old guidance counselor via phone in hopes that we could make some registration head way without actually being in person so that all I would need to do was sign a few things when I dropped her off for her classes. This was unfortunately not the case. She needed to be present, and I needed to do it all in person. Not via fax, email, phone, or snail mail. When we arrived at the school, her counselor was prepared for us. She had the paperwork ready for us to begin, however when I began to explain the situation to her, things became a bit more difficult, yet favorable on my end. Because it is district policy for the children to reside within the school district for the school that they will be attending, there was a need for proof of residency. When I explained to the madam that this could not happen, that although I owned property in the district, we no longer were residents in their district, let alone their state, she and her superiors were not pleased. I explained that as of three days prior, I was given a court order to return my daughter to her former school and the judge didn't care how this was to take place. My intentions were to commute her daily, for I had no other viable options as my parents, her grandparents, already had their hands full with their failing disabilities. Having her reside with family members was not an option. Even so, if it was, I had no family members who resided in the district either.

The office members were not sure how to handle our situation. Like me, they thought that the story seemed outrageous and ridiculous. The principal of the school was out of the facility until the following Monday. Thanks are to Jesus! I was given some more time to prepare my game plan. The principal said he would contact the district and their attorneys and get an answer back to me as soon as possible. I was confident that I had done what I could to stay on my own solid ground for the time being. I did not lie to the school officials about the fact that I still owned property within the district. I was sure to let them know of the entire situation. At any given time, just as I was worried about being so far away from my two smallest children, I would be just as far away from my oldest. She was still a child and needed someone reliable close to her if necessary as well.

It took just over a week and a half for me to receive an answer back from the school district. They denied her enrollment! I was enlightened once more. I was so thankful that God continued to be with me as I struggled with trying to grasp the entire situation as a whole. Unfortunately, I knew that there was no way that this wondrous miracle was going to be an end to all of my woes. I contacted my lawyer the next day and asked him what he suggested for me to do next. He entered a motion with the court asking the judge what he would like for us to do with the situation. Another trial date was set.

St. Patrick's Day was the chosen day to appear in court once again. Again, my daughter ran around with her "other" family like small children. She showed up in a mini skirt and her hair dyed green. She was dressed identically to her stepsisters. She presented herself as immature and disrespectful to the situation once again. I was embarrassed to say that I had raised her. The child that I knew that I had raised would have never shown up in such attire and behaved so poorly. Her stepmother was just as much of a pitiful sight as she was in her performances outside of the courtroom. She too, was loud with giggles and was chasing after the girls as if she were one of them. She represented herself not at all as a mature parental figure would want to display in public, especially during a child custody battle. My lawyer and I viewed the situation in awe trying not to judge them, but unable to keep from staring like the rest of the onlookers did in the courthouse hallway.

When it was finally time to go in, we entered quietly and sat at the two tables set up. One was for her father, as the Petitioner and the other one was for me, the Respondent.

It was almost impossible to not feel like a criminal as I approached the knee height door to enter the area designated for us and our attorneys. My palms immediately began to sweat in nervousness and I could feel a lump swell up in my throat. I felt completely out of place. To me, I was a law abiding citizen with a Christian soul and I had absolutely no business being inside a courtroom for any personal reasons. Once again, I could not believe that the events unfolding before me were playing a part in my history, in my story, or worse yet, the story of my little girl.

The judge entered the courtroom and the proceedings began. He heard from both sides regarding why the school district might have denied my daughter's enrollment. Our position stood on the grounds that the district regional superintendent would not allow the enrollment secondary to district policy. Our opposing side said that I did not do everything that I could have to ensure compliance in fulfilling the court order to have her enrolled because I explained to the office officials that although I still owned property in the area, we did not reside there. The judge could not believe that the school would go against a court order so he and the two attorneys went back into his chambers. The judge personally called the district's regional superintendent for himself.

I was not sure what to expect when the three came back out into the courtroom about fifteen minutes later. There were arguments from the superintendent that it is policy for the children to reside within the school district for which they reside. This meant that where the child lays his or her head from Sunday through Thursday needs to be near the school that they will attend. The rules are made for the best interest of the children. The judge took none of that into account and argued back that there was a standing court order for which the district was to honor. These were not their usual circumstances. So the district was forced to allow my daughter to attend and finish the spring semester. Nine weeks had passed by this time. I asked my lawyer to find out about the circumstances of her academics. What were we to do if her course credits didn't transfer? He replied, "That's her problem. She asked for all of this."

CHAPTER 6

GRABBING AHOLD

"Her problem" was his response? How could the academics of a fourteen year old girl be only her problem? She wasn't mature enough to think about her future. She didn't have much to deal with in the situation either. All she was going to have to do was attend the classes she was told to attend. I was the one who had to resume her enrollment again the following day. That meant transferring classes and dropping classes from her current high school. That part should have been fairly simple. But, it wasn't. Unfortunately, the classes from our small town did not match those of her old high school and that meant a lot of juggling. Her counselor and I worked diligently together to find the best alternatives. From the beginning of the process, she was only going to get credit for three of the seven classes that she was going to be taking. The classes she had started to take near home weren't transferring and it looked like the majority of her spring semester would have to be retaken again the following year or with some summer classes. She was also going to be taking classes but not getting credit for them just so she could be in school for the full day to allow me to commute back to work and back again.

Her counselor was certainly taking pity on me. She pulled every string that she could. By my daughter's second day back to school there, her counselor had managed to get her into some sophomore and senior classes to allow her to get credit for some of the classes that she had already worked hard for nine weeks. By her doing so, she was able to finagle the schedule around so much that there was only one class that was going to be audited, or not credited, that she would be taking. I was thankful to God for continuing to lay his blessings before us. Even in such a trying situation, when my focus was blurred away from Him, He continued to carry me.

In John 16:16, Jesus told his disciples, *"For a little while you won't see me, but after a while you will see me."* God has known even from the very beginning of time that there may be times in our lives when we might lose our focus on Him because our vision may be blurred by the distractions going on around us. Even in those times when we may have forgotten about Him, He has not forgotten about us! We are His children, like our children belong to us. When they forget about who we are because of the selfish world tranquilizing them from all directions, we always remember them. We always love them, just as God loves us.

I was reminded of that and gave my thanks that my daughter would not have to retake her entire freshman semester. But, there was still so much more of the situation to deal with than just her going back to her old school. I still had my youngest children to worry about as well. I still had my job to worry about. I still had my bills to worry about. I still had another hearing over custody to contend with as well. It was determined for me that I was going to have to commute my daughter back and forth daily and then back to work. I would spend eight hours on the road each day. I had no options for someone to meet me halfway or for family members to assist with the situation. In essence, the decision for the immediate time being was determined for me.

The next matter of business, and most important of all, came into play with my other two children. I had no idea what to do about not being there for them every morning before school or immediately afterwards. In order for me to get my oldest to school on time, I would need to make sure that the two of us were on the road no later than 5:30AM. That would mean either leaving the children at home and hiring someone to help with them before school, or getting all of us out of the house and having them to the sitter's before then. There was nine weeks of school left in the spring semester. I knew that my daycare provider did begin her day that early and sometimes my children did too. Still, the idea of my children rushing around so early and not getting their rest before school made me almost irate. Twelve hours a day away from my two youngest also made me furious. There was not one part of the situation that would not affect them somehow. It was hard for me not to be angry. The ire was already building up inside me like a fiery wall of flames. I officially viewed this as a war. I knew that my daughter was just a confused child. She was at a point in her life where she was just seeking some form of security and stability after everything that she had been through. In her mind, her stability was her friends. Still, I couldn't help being upset at her father for the upheaval that was being forced upon us as a family.

"Don't get so angry that you sin. Don't go to bed angry and don't give the devil a chance. If you are a thief, quit stealing. Be honest and work hard, so you will have something to give to people in need. Stop all your dirty talk. Say the right thing at the right time and help others by what you say. Don't make God's spirit sad. The Spirit makes you sure that someday you will be free from your sins. Stop being bitter and angry and mad at others. Don't yell at one another or curse each other or ever be rude. Instead, be kind and merciful, and forgive others, just as God forgave you because of Christ."

Ephesians 4:26-32

I kept my temper as calm as I could. In order to do so, my daughter and I rarely spoke of the situation. I knew that if we did then I would not be able to maintain my self control. I prayed daily to prevent myself from saying anything that might harm her emotionally. I really did understand how she was feeling. I just didn't like how it affected the rest of our family.

A friend of mine offered to stay with the little ones and help them off to school and pick them up at the end of the day. But hadn't the kids dealt with enough already? I wasn't given much time to think about the situation. It became one of the biggest blessings of all that he did.

After giving thanks for being my support system, I turned my attention towards my employer. The extra driving meant less availability for my on-site work. I wasn't sure how long I would be allowed to play the game of being so unavailable. My health insurance was also going to be at risk due to the decrease in my hours. I was still in the qualifying stages of eligibility for my insurance. I really couldn't afford to take the risk. I spoke with my supervisor. She agreed to give me some time to figure out what I needed to do to pull the situation together.

With everything set into a rough drafted plan, school resumed the following Monday morning. My daughter and I made the commute back and forth from Iowa to Illinois and back again for several days. I drove while she slept. I had plenty of time to think and rethink the entire scenario over and over again in my head. I juggled ideas, flipping them around in my head, trying to play the situation out as to which ones would give me the best options for saving time, saving money, making money, and allowing me to be with all of my children when they needed me. It seemed like an impossible mountain that I was determined to climb and to crush. I was not going to allow my story to play along the way that it was. I controlled the setting and I controlled the plot. God never said we would know which path we were on, only that if we had faith and followed Him, we could walk that path with confidence. I knew that God was guiding me to a corrective plan of action. I could feel His pull. I was ready to put that plan into action.

Although the corrective plan to the situation left a few faults of its own, it kept my priorities in place. After dropping my daughter off at school one morning, I met with my ex-husband to discuss the details of our situation and what I was planning on doing with it. Together, we decided that it would be best for all of the children involved if I moved them back, temporarily, to their old home (where he was currently living) and back to their old school. My job was already frustrated with my "in and out" status. They were also seeking corrective action. All I needed to do next was to make some phone calls to set things in place to get us through the next eight weeks of a ridiculous court order.

Every time I tell this story, I feel like crawling into a hole and hiding. Unfortunately, I **had** to tell everyone at least part of the story in order for them to understand why after only ten weeks, I was going to temporarily relocate my family again. I also had to make sure everyone was aware that we would be returning to the schools in our little town, so that they would not close out all of our files there either. It was hard to let everyone outside of my very personal circle hear what was happening to my family. But I couldn't focus on that. I had to keep my attention on what was presented before me. I couldn't worry about the judgments of others. More often than not, everyone else was in just as much awe over the situation as I was.

My first phone call was to the private Catholic school that my youngest children had attended. We had previously received grant assistance for help with tuition. I was hopeful that the tuition amount would remain the same. Their school was happy to accept them back on the same terms for which they left. I set a start date for them to begin within a couple of days. Secondly, I contacted my old babysitter so see if she still had a place for my son in her care. It was affirmative once again. Thirdly, I contacted my employer and offered to work a weekend package which consisted of working anywhere to twenty to thirty hours between Friday,

Saturday, and Sunday. This would mean only one day after school away from my kids, and their dads could be the ones who looked after them. This offer gave me more time on site to treat my patients and saved me a lot of money in gas. I would stay away over the weekends and be with the kids during the week. It wasn't totally ideal, but it was a much better option than the previous one that I was in.

The next item on the agenda was to nail down the schedule with everyone else involved. My parents agreed that my oldest and I could stay with them overnight during the week. My youngest two would stay with their dad in our old house. Because he had to work at 6AM that still meant that we would need to leave my parents house in the early morning hours to be there for the little ones. That was okay with me because that meant that only she and I were being put out and not the smaller kids. I made all of my other calls to current schools, my daycare provider, and to cancel the spring sports that the kids were signed up for. The end goal was that I needed to keep my family together. I was a mom to all three of my children. I had to know that I was there for each and every one of them.

My friend back home and I discussed the situation in length. He said he understood and agreed to hold down the fort at my home, feeding the dogs, maintaining the house and yard, etc. He was set on his agenda. I was set on mine. The kids and I moved back to Illinois that following weekend.

CHAPTER 7

MAKING THE CLIMB

"Don't be worried! Have faith in God and have faith in me. There are many rooms in my Father's house. I wouldn't tell you this, unless it was true. I am going there to prepare a place for each of you. After I have done this, I will come back and take you with me. Then we will be together. You know the way to where I am going."

John 14:1-4

This became a further reminder from Jesus that no matter where we were in this world, God was with us. From our small cabin-like house back to our castle, He had followed us back and forth along the way. It didn't matter which house we were landing at each time, He was always there making us always feel at home. It did become a bit confusing for the kids at times when we had to make references to the word "home" and they would ask questions like "which home?". I was getting a first-hand experience of what my children were experiencing. Their confusion was also mine. We were "home" at both places. We hadn't had much of a chance to make our "cabin" feel like home yet. We were back in our old house, with our old rooms, with our old appliances, with our old neighbors, and with their daddy. It was home. So, how was I going to get my children to adjust to their new home when I was forced to keep them at their old one? It was all very confusing and God was heavily speaking to my heart. I just couldn't understand everything that he was saying.

If ever my ex-husband and I were going to rethink our decision to divorce, that would have been the time to do it. It was like God was saying, "You moved too haste. You left things unfinished here. There is more to think about. There is more to settle. Back up. Here is your old life back, just for a moment. Here is your house; here is your family; here is your husband."

I was not prepared for the flood of emotions that began to overwhelm me. We had not moved back for those reasons. We had moved back to keep our family, me and my children, together. My ex-husband was not supposed to be a part of that. But, he was an enormous part of that circle. It was confusing to all five of us. The kids were happy to have everyone back in the same house together. We weren't miserable living together again either. We didn't fight at all. We actually found each other to be very supportive towards each other regarding the whole situation. My daughter was his daughter too, or at least he had raised her as his daughter for the last ten years. He loved her every bit as much as he did his other two children. With the divorce, he was now without any rights to her and she was a rebellious teenager forgetting all that he had done for her. She had neglected to remember all the times that he was there for every game and every dance recital in which her biological father was not. She had forgotten when he stayed home for her when she was sick or when he stayed up late so she could be with friends. He was just as upset and worried about the outcome of the situation as I was. He too did not want to see our daughter get herself into a situation that she would regret for the rest of her life.

He also put extra effort into being there with the other two children so that I could work the weekends. Even though his visitation was not technically for every weekend, he wanted to have as much time with them as he could have with them. He seemed to appreciate them just a little bit more than he did before. He was glad to have his kids closer to him in miles again. It meant a lot more time with them for him, which we were all thankful for. Moving the kids so far from him and the rest of our family was a very difficult thing for me to do.

My oldest daughter and I had only stayed with my parents for a few nights before we decided to stay at our old house with everyone else. My ex was working late and leaving early, and we were staying later and getting there early in the morning. It made it easier on everyone. I felt like we were putting my parents out because when we were there, my dad graciously gave us his bed to sleep in and he slept on the couch. We would arrive late and he would stay up later than he usually did to wait for us. Our things were scattered between the two houses and pulling things from the suitcases daily was inconvenient at best. It saved a lot of time and energy over all by staying with my ex. To this day, I am still thankful for his hospitality throughout the situation.

Once we were back in Illinois full-time, I jumped right back into helping with the little ones at their school and my middle daughter resumed soccer with her old team. The kids were comfortable. My job was working out well with the weekend hours. I was even able to get some extra hours in with another company that had part time work locally. My budget was still sacrificing, but my ex-husband took the bills over for our old house and I gave him a verbal agreement to repay him for my half of the debt when I could.

I had reason to hope. 1 Peter 5-7 tells us that it is ok to have that hope. It says, *"Your faith will be like gold that has been tested with fire. And these trials will prove that your faith is worth much more than gold that can be destroyed. They will show that you will be given praise and honor and glory when Jesus Christ returns."* The scriptures are telling us that our faith may be tested. Our trust and respect for Him and for others might be in question. But don't let it be destroyed. I continued to hold true to my belief in Him, knowing He would someday praise us and bring us glory. As long as I continued to hold on to my hopes and dreams, the promises for a life of receiving His bounty would surely be ours to hold onto forever. All I had to do was continue to believe that we were only inches away from finishing the climb onto the mountains and boulders in front of us.

I held onto that hope and continued to do what we had always done. The kids settled in and little was said much more from my daughter about her wishes to go live with her father. She was happy to be with her friends. She had openly admitted to several people including me, other family members, and a therapist that her whole reasoning for seeking the change of custody was so that she could remain in the same school with her peers. I kept the understanding in my heart that she was seeking the stability and solidity in the only place where she at the time felt like she knew where to find it. Her friends had in essence to her became a part of her extended family. One of her girlfriends had spent the majority of the past summer living with us and the two of them had become inseparable. She was now feeling the peace of her calmer ground. She was feeling the "normalcy" return back to her life. She was hopeful that she had reversed the situational effects of my divorce on her in its entirety.

My kids were happy to have me available to them as I had always been. I was able to volunteer at their school, stay home more with my son, and stage our house for sale. We were kept on our toes with sports and chasing after an active young toddler. The staging process of presenting our house as totally obtainable, affordable, attractive, and comfortable, proceeded on with my full determination. Every time I came back on the weekends from "home" after working I brought with me some decorative pieces to spice up the place. The house had taken the form of a bachelor pad after the kids and I moved out and my ex moved back in. So, I bought a few "show pieces" as well to compliment the ones I brought with me to appeal to the women who would be walking through the house. I was determined to make them "ooh" and "aah" over the décor and make the buyers picture themselves living in my house. My efforts paid off. By the end of the spring semester, we had a signed contract for the sale of our house.

It was the end of May. I was looking forward to closing so many chapters in our lives and moving forward with the new hopes and dreams that I had began to envision myself working towards in the beginning of the year. The first chapter to close was the end of the spring semester for all three children. The judge had ordered us to only return for the spring semester. After that, I had filed a motion to remove her to the state of Iowa. Chapter one was closed. The little ones had the chance to say goodbye to their friends and finish out the school year as well giving them a longer and more complete closure. My ex husband and I had finally, after just over five months, sold our house. Chapter two was closed. I never again had to look back and wonder if we had made the right decision because we had discussed the "what if's" of the situation over and over. We were satisfied with our decision to remain separate but on the same team. The two of us had also had our closure. It left us now better parents and the best of friends. Chapter three was now closed. It was Memorial Day weekend, and I was finally free to move on…for good.

CHAPTER 8

ANOTHER CHAPTER

I patiently waited, Lord, for you to hear my prayer. You listened and pulled me from a lonely pit full of mud and mire. You let me stand on a rock with my feet firm, and you gave me a new song, a song of praise to you.

Psalm 40:1-3

We were finally in Iowa full-time. There would be no more judgments made to return back to Illinois to finish out the school year. Summer was finally underway. We made our final move back to our small cabin and resumed the plans that we had started to do a few months earlier. My daughter had made no more comments about returning back to Illinois and she began to re-establish the relationships she had with her old friends. She enrolled in a driver's education class and got her learner's permit. Her friendships seemed strong and she was scarcely home without company in tow. She volunteered to help out at my son's daycare several days per week to keep herself busy during the day hours when her friends were at cheerleading and football practices. She was appearing to be comfortable in her new environment.

The little ones were also enjoying the peace. They were finally aware of where their new home was and what it meant to be there. They were meeting new friends and enjoying the community's activities. They didn't ask anymore about returning to their old house or their old school. They settled into their environment as if they had been there for years. They had a fresh taste of what it meant to live in a small town and to see all of their peers everywhere they went. Although my finances suffered terribly with all that had happened, I was able to keep them happy with outings to the local YMCA, church events, zoo, and multiple parks that the area had to offer.

While the kids and I were away, my friend had fixed up the basement of our rental. He finished the walls, and laid down a cheap linoleum floor so that we could utilize the space when we returned. He also fixed up the rest of the place, patching holes, painting, spraying for bugs, trimming trees, fixing gutters, and things of the like. His presence while I was away was priceless. It was so easy to see how comforting and supportive a small town could be through the friends and people that had helped me to deal with our situation. Although I had lived in our town for several years before, I was amazed at how differently the people of the community were willing to go the extra mile to help me out with something that seemed so small to them, yet so enormous to us. We were finally able to feel like it was home again.

My job was also thankful for my full-time return, and my career was taking off. I was able to start to slowly pay off the doubled bills for both properties that had piled up during my misfortunate upheaval. Every dime I made was unfortunately gone before it was ever received. Finally in June, I received my unemployment payout.

"Trust the Lord and live right! The land will be yours, and you will be safe. Do what the Lord wants, and he will give you your heart's desire. Let the Lord lead you and trust him to help. Then it will be clear as the noonday sun that you were right. Be patient and trust the Lord. Don't let it bother you when all goes well for those who do sinful things."

Psalm 37:3-7

The scriptures tell us that if we are patient then good things will come. I had waited and believed in myself. I knew that the reasoning for being let go from my job was not for anything that I had done wrong. The fight to receive my unemployment benefits might have been a lingering battle, but God knew what He was doing. I was right in the thick of heavy debt from being unable to work full-time because of my situation with my daughter. That money could not have come at a better time. It didn't amount to much, but it was something.

June and July flew by without a glitch. The beginning of August rolled about and the kids were all talking about the start of a new school year. I still hadn't heard anything about another court date, and happily enrolled my children in the local schools. About a week after registration, the letter came. There was another date set for the child custody and visitation hearing. It was scheduled for the first day of school. My heart sank. My daughter had mentioned nothing about it to me. She had dropped no hints or comments. She kept her defiant secrets to herself. She knew full well that these plans were always in the mix and kept them hidden from me to avoid any altercations.

I contacted my attorney's office to find out why I was not notified of the hearing any sooner and to see if we could postpone the date so that the kids would not have to miss their first day of school. My lawyer said we could not delay the date. I could not believe that I had to go through everything again. I had just gotten home. I had just promised my job I was there full-time. I had promised myself that I could now give the kids the stability that they deserved. I had already risked so much already. I couldn't understand how my daughter could continue to pursue such a selfish act after I had given up so much to keep us all together. I couldn't believe that she couldn't see how much she meant to me after all that I had done to prove to her that I would never give up on her. I couldn't believe that she didn't know that her family was more important than her friends. I was irate. I was hurt. I was lost.

"Before I could get my breath, my miseries would multiply"
Job 9:18

It seemed like everything that I had fought so hard to achieve had just been washed away once again. My first born, the daughter that I had always been so proud of, was choosing her friends over her family. She was choosing to be with "Disney" parents who would play like they were teenagers themselves and spend her step mom's mother's money on vacations that they could not afford on their own. She admittedly, was choosing to be where the grass (or money) looked greener on the other side. Honestly, I'm not sure what teenager wouldn't prefer that kind of life. Instead of a life filled with integrity, lessons on how to scrimp and save, family, and church, she wanted something happier. She wanted fun and friends and money to do as she pleased. She wanted what I could no longer offer her now that I was divorced. I did not blame her for it. I was angry and I was hurt. But I didn't blame her. I let my daughter know how I felt about the situation. She knew in her heart that it was wrong. But still, she was being led by Satan's temptations.

"Don't hold grudges. On the other hand, it's wrong not to correct someone who needs correcting. Stop being angry and don't try to take revenge." Then in Proverbs 22:6 and 22:15 we are told, *"Teach your children right from wrong, and when they are grown they will still do right....All children are foolish, but firm correction will make them change."*

Leviticus 19:17-18

CHAPTER 9

THE TUMBLE

QUESTIONING GOD

"Dear friends, don't be surprised or shocked that you are going through testing that is like walking through fire. Be glad for the chance to suffer as Christ suffered. It will prepare you for even greater happiness when he makes his glorious return."
1 Peter 4:12-13

I prayed over and over selfishly for God to keep my first born with me. I worried that she would be led into trouble if she would be allowed to go with her father. He was an openly stated atheist and they had already taught her so much about defiance since January when she first began her lies and sneaking around. I worried that he did not know enough about her to be able to control her behaviors or to see her worries. I worried that he was making her promises again that he had no intentions of keeping. He was still promising her school in Illinois which would be a promise impossible for him to keep as long as he lived in Iowa. She believed him anyway.

August 25, 2010 was the final court date and my daughter was subpoenaed to testify. I was expected to drive her there. Two hours of silence filled the car as the blacktop passed underneath us. She listened to her iPod and we drove. I sat staring out the window with my palms sweating from silent nervousness. My ex husband made the opposite journey to Iowa to share with the kids in my other daughter's first day of second grade and to spend the day with our son. It felt like we had to walk a mile when we arrived at the courthouse. Each step bludgeoning with the weight of my heart making my stomach more and more vile. Although the weather outside was warm and breezy, I was boiling internally. The walk towards the building knowing what was in my future, made me unnoticeably perspire even more. Within seconds of arrival, my daughter immediately targeted the Jeep of her father and step mother and jumped into their vehicle without saying another word to me. I continued to make my way into the courthouse as if the parking lot was filled with quick sand. Each step forced, focused, and suffocating my soul.

Once again, feeling like a criminal, I set my purse and files through the conveyor and stepped through the metal detector. After being cleared, I headed upstairs to find the courtroom and to meet with my attorney. To my surprise, I had no idea that there would be a witness and testimony sort of hearing. My daughter was asked to remain outside of the courtroom, as well as her step mother, so that the two of them could also be "key witnesses" in the trial. The hearing began and the three of them were eventually asked a series of questions regarding their cause. They were asked questions about me and my parenting skills. To my surprise, as I was waiting for the daggers to fly, there were none. They all held to their story that my daughter wanted to stay in the area with her dad and her stepsisters so that she could see them more. They all mentioned very little about her fight for her stay with her friends or her change to a completely different school district. Her dad admitted to tax fraud throwing the judge for a bit of a loop, but for which she overlooked in order to stay focused on the situation at hand. Her step mom stated that she could not remember whether or not my daughter was even a part of their Christmas gathering just eight months before. Both parents stated that her dad would rarely be around and that it was her step mom who would do the majority of the child rearing.

The questions that were asked to me, were not what I expected either. I was asked about how little he took care of her or how much he was there for her in the past. I was asked about my job and how many jobs I used to work beginning when I was seventeen. I am guessing those questions were to prove that I had always taken on all financial responsibility for my daughter. I was asked about the kind of student she was and what her personality was like. I was asked nothing about why I felt like she should stay with the person who had raised her for her entire life. The questions were all very short and to the point.

The judge made no decision that day and we were forced to go home and wait out her thoughts on the matter. I called my attorney's office the next day and there was still no decision. The waiting game was killing me. I felt good about how the trial had gone. I felt like all three of them had hung themselves. My daughter had lied and said that she didn't remember not seeing her dad for five months. Her father admitted to never being around and to tax fraud. Her step mother couldn't even remember if my daughter was there with them for the holidays. I was proven to be a very fit parent and had always been in her life. I was almost certain that things were going to come out in my favor. I was sure that my daughter was going to see that she was meant to be home with her mother and that she could finally relax and find herself again.

That afternoon, I began picking up the kids at school just as I always had. As the children got in the car and we began to make our way home, my daughter's phone immediately began to blow up with the buzzing vibrations of text messages. This time was different. This time she read her messages and dialed an outgoing call. From the back seat in a giddy "Really?!!" with tears rolling down her face. I got the answer that I had prayed that I would never in my life have to hear. She had won. She was going to leave, still as a child, and there was nothing that I could do about it. Right then and right there, I died inside.

"Don't trample prisoners under your feet or cheat anyone out of what is rightfully theirs. God Most High sees everything, and he knows when you refuse to give someone a fair trial."
Lamentations 3:34-38

I immediately became disconnected from all reasoning and self worth. My family was oblivious to the thoughts that were spinning inside my head. My daughter eagerly hurried upstairs to her bedroom while I got the little ones a snack. I made my way around the house in a fury gathering clothes and toys and trinkets to pack into suitcases for my little ones. I sent my ex-husband a message to meet me at our usual halfway spot and filled him in briefly on the verdict. I knew nothing more about the verdict but my daughter's giggles ringing within my ears. But I knew that I could not handle myself as a composed mother towards my small and innocent children that night. I knew that I would have to be alone. All I felt was nausea and sorrow in my gut. I loaded up the children and took them to meet with my ex-husband. I said my goodbyes to them without the intention of ever seeing them again. At that point in my life, I felt the fight was gone in me. I was done, wanting nothing else in this world to cut and tear and absolutely shred at my heartstrings ever again. I had no more will. I was irrationally thinking that I had lost them too. I felt like a prisoner in my own world.

"I am a follower of Christ, and the Holy Spirit is a witness to my conscience. So I tell the truth and I am not lying when I say my heart was broken and I am in great sorrow."

Romans 9:1-2

Within a few minutes, my dear friend came over. He didn't realize what had transpired that afternoon, only what was supposed to be coming into process. I was hysterically bawling and hyperventilating. I could not control my emotions. I felt like my daughter had just died, was murdered right before my eyes. I wanted to die with her. He did his best to console me, but I was heartbroken. We cried together and he finally talked me into leaving her room. We made our way downstairs and I headed into the bathroom. My head was throbbing. I was spinning in circles. My reasoning was out of control. I could feel my pulse inside my head and the spasms radiating from it firing and piercing inside my skull. My vision was already beginning to blur and my speech began to slur in the midst of my broken breaths. My physical medical condition was at one of its absolute worst phases and my psychological condition was even worse. I locked the door behind me and grabbed several bottles of prescription pills, clutching them fist in hand. I knelt down on the cold tiled floor, rocking myself back and forth, back and forth. With a cup of water, I stared at my chosen my poisons. Back and forth. Back and forth. Back and forth I rocked staring at the pipe underneath of my sink.

I envisioned my children without me and how much happier I thought that they would be. I saw my ex-husband confused and pale with tears streaming down his cheeks. I saw myself watching my daughter grow up, misled, as I was a ghostly figure. I saw myself following her every move but still never being able to keep her out of harm's way. I saw that my parents saw understanding in how hurt I must have felt. I saw my dad trying to console my daughter so that she would not feel at fault in the situation. I saw my funeral. I pictured only my immediate family and my ex. My children were not there so that they were protected from the memory. The friends that I had thought were my friends were too busy to attend. I felt absolutely alone in my death just as I had felt at that moment in my life. I prayed for God to take my soul. I wondered where He was as I lifted a capful of pills and put them in my mouth. Then, I choked. I was scared and panic stricken. Just as I leaned over the toilet, I heard my friend as he called out to me from the other room. I began to weep.

Isaiah 30:19 says, *"People of Jerusalem, you don't need to cry anymore. The Lord is kind, and as soon as He hears your cries for help, He will come. The Lord has given you trouble and sorrow as your food and drink. But now you will again see the Lord, your teacher, and He will guide you. Whether you turn to the right or to the left, you will hear a voice saying, "This is the road! Now follow it."*

God heard my cries. He knew I had had all that I could have put on my shoulders and that I was now struggling for everything that I believed in. I was struggling for what was right and what was wrong. I was struggling to save my life. As I pushed myself back away from my porcelain thrown, I met troubled eyes with my partner. He had unlocked the door to find me swallowed up in my own misery. I had tried so hard to hide my anguish from him and from everyone else. But, he walked right into the thick center of my quicksand. I could see his worry written all over his brow from where I lay my head on the cool hard floor. He knelt down beside me and picked up the open bottles to see what they contained. With a gasp, and a cry, he picked me up and carried me away.

I fell asleep that night still hoping to never wake up again. My voicemail and text boxes continued to fill up with calls from family and friends. I could not bear to respond to any of them. The next morning, I was left alone. I lay on my living room floor, where my "bed" had been for the last eight months since moving to the cabin. I was surrounded by pillows and I was wrapped up in two of the quilts that I had made. I was propped with things warm and comfortable, but I still felt so cold and empty. My phone rang close to 7:30 AM. It was my daycare provider, and a very good friend. I knew she was only wondering if my son was coming over for the day. I didn't want to not call and not show up for I knew she would worry. I answered my phone for the first time in two days.

She could hear the grief that was stricken in my voice. My words trembled and flubbed as I sobbed out the story of losing my daughter. I cried to her about never again being able to take her to school or pick her up again. I cried over never seeing the worry in her face as she struggled to study for her exams. I cried over wonder if she really knew how much I loved her. My girlfriend is such an angel in every life that she blesses. She was able to get me to momentarily stop wallowing in my one horrible circumstance and remind me of my other two children. Over the phone, as I grieved my loss, she prayed out loud for me. She told me of the importance of who I was in my children's lives and assured me that someday, my oldest would return her heart back to mine. I wasn't convinced; but I was listening. She told me she was worried that I may try to do something stupid. She asked me to promise her that those thoughts were not inside my head. I couldn't and I somehow managed to elude the question and we ended our conversation. It was a lot for me to take in. I closed my eyes and drifted back off to sleep.

Soon, I got another call from another friend. I did not answer, allowing it to go to voicemail. Her message was just as sweet. I had barely spoken to her since my move back to Iowa or my move from Iowa to Illinois to Iowa again. I listened to it feeling ashamed. Her message was very upbeat telling me to hang in there and that she and her family would be praying for me. Then I could hear the break in her voice. She caught herself, regrouped, and finished the message with her blessings. It wasn't really what she had said, or the upbeat "get back in the game" kind of thing that I felt with her message. It was the break in her tone. It was the "I remember her as a little girl growing up with mine" and the "It's ok, because this really is awful" message that the break in the tone of her voice told me.

I spoke with a couple of other friends of mine and also with my dad. My ex called several times throughout the day, knowing that I would always answer his calls because the kids were with him. I was still trying to swallow everything that had been shoveled down my throat in such a short time. I was still trying to make myself get up off of the floor and make the decision to press forward. I was still trying to convince myself to get out of my own shoes and for a few moments, put on the shoes of my other children so that I could remember how much they had already suffered.

"And just as God raised Jesus, he will also raise us to life. Then he will bring us into his presence…"
2 Corinthians 13

That powerful day was a day of realization for me. I realized that I am not defined by my mistakes. I couldn't do it alone or pretend to anymore. There was no shame in my suffering and no healing in my silent self torment. The world was moving on without me. I had to somehow let go of my losses and move on. Jesus was giving me the power to pick myself back up and bring myself back to life. I crawled off of my floor and I began putting into place the powers of recovery. 2 Corinthians 17 says, *"Anyone who belongs to Christ is a new person. The past is forgotten, and everything is new."* The structure of my self worth had crumbled and I was determined to rebuild it on a stronger foundation. I promised myself that my losses would be remembered as a fight with dignity and respect and with love and effort. I was going to regroup and move forward forgiving those who fought against me and letting go of the past in order to find peace. I decided to continue to follow the scriptures as I was told to do it in 1 Peter 3:9. That is, *"Don't be hateful and insult people just because they are hateful and insult you. Instead, treat everyone with kindness."* I picked up the remnants of my broken heart and handed them back over to Christ. I prayed for Him to continue to hold my right hand and to be my strength. When I felt my feet slipping, as they often did, He continued to come to steady me with His love. When I was worried, He continued to comfort me and make me feel secure.

CHAPTER 10

FINDING HOME

"I am sure that what we are suffering now cannot compare with the glory that will be shown to us"

Romans 8:18

The promises of Jesus continue to present themselves in my life every day. Although I was stricken with a burden of worry and heartache, there was also a flood of unanswered prayers that came after each trial that I have encountered in my life. I have learned what it is like to be humble and to be thankful for the things that I do have. Although money has never been abundant, it has taught not only me, but my children, the value in a more frugal lifestyle. I have learned to be strong and to hold my head high. I care not about the judgement of others. My story is not theirs, and theirs will never be mine. God gave me my thumbprint. It is like no one else's. I have learned to turn my hands over to Christ and to feel the freedom of knowing that I do not have to climb any mountain on my own. I am not expected to be without flaw and I can only do my best. We all have to learn to carry ourselves. Our health and happiness starts with us first.

After my daughter moved, I was able to rededicate my attention to my two younger children and put more effort into their lives. My middle daughter is now a beautiful young teenager, blooming into a bold and beautiful personality. She has kept me very proud and busy with school sports and activities. My son was later diagnosed with Autism and in his younger years needed more significant attention and understanding to meet his needs. The amount of focus needed would have been even more difficult while maintaining attention to my oldest daughter who was a teenager at that time. I have been able to put more effort into my work and into my own selfish ambitions. My daughter and I kept a relatively close relationship. Within a year, I was able to buy a vehicle and a new home. We made new friends, were thankful for old, and we re-established a life back in our community. Eventually, just as we are promised in *Psalm 146:8, "The Lord sets prisoners free and heals blind eyes. He gives a helping hand to everyone who fails."*, my daughter did find her way back home.

"I tell you not to worry about your life! Don't worry about having something to eat or wear. Life is more than food or clothing. Look at the crows! They don't plant or harvest and they don't have storehouses or barns. But God takes care of them. You are much more important than any birds. Can worry make you live longer? If you don't have power over small things, why worry about everything else? Look how the wild flowers grow!

They don't work hard to make their clothes. But I tell you that Solomon with all his wealth wasn't as well clothed as one of these flowers. God gives such beauty to everything that grows in the fields, even though it is here today and thrown into a fire tomorrow. Won't he do even more for you? You have such little faith! Don't keep worrying about having something to eat or drink. Only people who don't know God are always worrying about such things. Your Father knows what you need. But put God's work first and these things will be yours as well."

Luke 12:22-30

I have learned that there is nothing in this world that I have to conquer on my own. There is always someone on my team no matter how alone I feel. I may not be rich in possessions or money. I may not be rich in clothes or have a feast at my table. But I am rich in friends, and even richer in Christ's love and in my faith in Him. I will never worry again about where we will live or how I will provide for my family, because It says in His word that he is my source and supplier! We have heard the term "God will only give you what he knows that you can handle". He must have thought I am one hell of a woman to put so much in front of me all at once! I know I didn't think I would make it out. No matter how large these obstacles may have been, or how big they may have seemed, they were not impossible. I am here. I learned and recognized too much in my life to be thankful for. No matter how heavy and time consuming things are to move, they are not impossible for us to overcome. They are just the rocks that we use as our stepping stones for the mountains that we have to climb. With every bead of sweat that rolls off of our brow as we climb, pull and step, scrape, and weep, we are that much closer to reaching the top of our mountain. Our destination is the path that He has chosen for us. Just because there is a cloud obstructing our view, doesn't mean we should stop. We will never know if we are only one more step away from our goals and from our destiny if we don't keep on climbing. When we do finally reach the top, we never forget how we learned how to grip onto God's strength harder and what it felt like to feel a tighter hold in His hand during our journey there. We will know that through our faith, and our faith alone, all of our tribulations have been achieved and all of our trials have been overcome. We will know that we were not judged by how we learned God's word along the way or by how quickly we got there. We will only be judged on how we followed His word. With Christ as our guide, we can then step onto those mountains and kick down the boulders and we'll use them for the next stepping stones in our climb. Eventually, we will have peace within ourselves, peace with others, and peace with God. There won't be anymore mountains and we can take those boulders and break them down a little at a time, crushing each one into tiny pea gravel there are hundreds of small stones. How we look at life is solely up to us. But how we receive life's blessings is up to God. When we are done with our journey, we can use the gravel of our stories to beautifully landscape the dreams that we have received through God's precious bounty or we can use it to become a jagged edge, like a rock in our shoe, that throws us continually off balance. I believe that God has a bigger plan. Our trials and experiences gives us strength to endure and our blessings build our faith. If I would have succeeded in ending my story when I wanted to, I would have never known that my daughter would come back home. I would have never bought my home on my own or shared my story with you. Your story is not over either. Your landscape is not finished. Remember, that not all blessings come easy. Even some flowers and bushes have protective thorns. It doesn't make them any less beautiful or produce less fruit.

"Learn to be patient, so that you will please God and be given what he has promised. As the Scriptures say,

"God is coming soon! It won't be very long. The people God accepts will live because of their faith. But he isn't pleased with anyone who turns back."

We are not like those people who turn back and get destroyed. We will keep on having faith until we are saved."

Hebrews 10:36-39

REFERENCES

American Bible Society, The Holy Bible Contemporary English Version. American Bible Society, 1995.

Printed in the United States
By Bookmasters